A Diary of Unfaithful Stories

ISBN: 978-1-917601-13-9

A Diary of Unfaithful Stories

Lora Kay

Also by Lora Kay

Darkness in the Light: short stories
A Woman

*To my closest friends, without whom
I would have given up countless times,
and whose love and support are as
unconditional as that of a family.*

The Beginning

I was only six years old when I was first introduced to the act of 'cheating'. My father held my hand as we walked to the post office – back in those days, people still sent letters to each other. 'This is our little secret, okay?' he said to me, hoping his young daughter would understand that this little outing wasn't to be shared with her mother. Unfortunately, for him, I was not familiar with the concept of lying just yet, and I ratted him out. Little did I know that my big mouth would put an end to my parents' marriage; my mother found the love letters that my father had been exchanging with another woman for quite some time.

I had to grow up carrying the guilt of telling my mother before eventually swapping that guilt for hatred towards my father for ruining our family and for putting something on my shoulders that I could not have possibly understood.

Eventually, I entered my teenage years and started dealing with feelings of love for the first time. Like many other young people going through this stage of life, I'd felt the pain of fancying someone who didn't fancy me back. This was the moment I realised that love was a complicated thing, and I decided that it might be time to reconsider the hate I felt for my father – I decided to understand him. After all, if love was complicated for me, a teenage girl, it was probably complicated for adults as well.

Yes, I did try to be the bigger person, the mature person, the one who had outgrown her age and was capable of forgiveness and letting go of pain. I only prayed that, one day, I would find real love and avoid the drama that happened in my family.

My father had left us to marry the woman he'd been seeing, his mistress. I guessed she was his real soulmate, and as painful as it was for me to accept, I felt rather grown up and a bit proud of myself for achieving this inner peace after years of anger and sadness within my child's heart. Yes, that was the feeling, until we later found out that my father was cheating on his second wife, too. Back to square one.

So, his mistress wasn't his real soulmate, then. It wasn't about mistaking my mother to be the right person for him; it wasn't about any of the mature justifications I'd made to explain his actions. So, what was it about then? What was the reason for cheating?

It wasn't just my family. As I became an adult, I came across many examples of the same sad story, shared through friends, acquaintances and so on; one would think I'd have found, or at least have been circling, the answer to my question – why do people cheat? But despite all this exposure, the reason for it all had only become more unclear.

At first, I was terrified of having this terrible thing happen to me. The fear made me alert, in a state of near-constant suspicion, mixed, of course, with jealousy. I didn't want to be anyone's second choice. I didn't want to share my first-place spot with anyone. I didn't want to be replaced as though I were no longer worthy of love and attention. Insecurity is a terrible thing to feel, for anyone, and despite my efforts to set myself free from the chains

I'd put on myself, fear always prevailed. My attempts to apply logical thinking would always be overpowered by childhood memories, resulting in a resurgence of insecurity and self-consciousness. Sad picture, but it was my state of being at this stage of my early life.

I swore I would never forgive cheating, and most importantly that I would never cheat. I was resolute until the moment I did, in fact, swallow my pride and forgive cheating, until I crossed my own principles and cheated myself. The saying 'never say never' took on a visceral new meaning for me.

Some people may analyse the meaning of the word 'cheating' and arrive at a judgement: a dishonourable act of disrespect and betrayal resulting in destruction and pain. Who would want that? Why would somebody choose this? I'd always thought it was straightforward, really. But the truth is – and this may be the closest I've come to anything resembling an answer for the motive – judging based on the act rather than the definition of the word is a little bit more complicated.

March 2011

There was no civil ring of the doorbell; someone was banging on my door, heavy and angry banging, and what made it even scarier was the fact that it was almost midnight. I tiptoed to the peephole, holding my phone, ready to dial 911, but the tension quickly diffused when I saw it was just my friend Melisa. I exhaled, thanking the universe there was no real danger, but after the fear passed, I was ready to kill my crazy friend for nearly giving me a heart attack.

'What the hell is …' I started as I unlocked the door, but Melisa didn't give me a chance to continue.

'Son of a bitch!' She stormed in as if it were her house and headed straight for the kitchen where she could light a cigarette, leaving me looking after her, confused and still holding the door open.

Melisa was known to have a bit of a radical temper – it was part of her charm – but I could sense there was something serious going on, something more. I hurried to lock the door and joined her in the kitchen where she was already sitting, a string of smoke coming off her cigarette, waiting for me. It looked like she'd already poured herself a coffee as well. Yes, she was quite comfortable. I wasn't irritated by this, even though we weren't best friends; in fact, I was amused more than anything.

'Who pissed you off so bad? Was it Tom?' I asked as I sat across from her.

'This mother fucker, Tom, yes of course it's him! It's always him. Who else would it be? Oh, were you about to go to bed?' she asked, looking at my pyjamas.

'Actually, yes, but this is more important – go on,' I smiled, only lightly laughing at the lateness of her observation.

'I'm sorry, honey, but you'll understand me once you hear what I've got to say.' The cigarette in her hand proceeded to burn itself down to a stub as Melisa told her story, too preoccupied to remember to smoke. 'I was in the neighbourhood, and as I was walking, a car passed by me on the street, a familiar car, Tom's car. And guess what? There was a woman sitting in the passenger seat! So – you know me – I decided I'd go over to his place and check on him. I was only ten minutes away anyway.'

'But why didn't you call first?' I interrupted.

She gave me a look that said I was mad even to suggest that.

'So he could lie to me over the phone? No, honey, that's not how you deal with such situations; you have to confront the bastard face to face!' She finally realised her cigarette had burnt out and stubbed it in the ashtray, lighting up a new one and giving me a second chance to get to the point she was trying to make. 'As I was walking, I was mentally swearing at him and that bitch he was with, imagining how I'd catch them together and beat the crap out of them once I'd seen it with my eyes.'

'How were you so sure it was his car, and him in there with that woman?' I just had to ask. The whole thing made no sense to me. I couldn't understand how she could jump to such a crazy conclusion just because she saw the same make and model of car that her boyfriend had. Her entire assumption was crossing the line, and ridiculousness, which I wouldn't dare to say out loud, of course, but still, I sit back and say nothing.

'Well, I caught him cheating before, so he lost the right to the benefit of the doubt, honey,' she said, voice low with the weight of a bitter past. I wanted to propose that she, perhaps, should consider ending it then and there rather than agonising in a continuing relationship with no trust, but her reasons for staying with him were her own – it wasn't my place to judge.

She continued, 'Eventually, I reached the building and noticed that his car was parked in front, in the usual parking spot. Thank God my brain was moving quickly and I thought to check if the car felt warm.'

'Why?'

'Good God, girl, you are so naïve. Seriously?' She gave me a suspicious look. 'If he'd driven the car recently, it'd still be warm – it would take a while to cool off. The only problem was that I had no idea how long it usually takes.'

'So what did you do?' I could feel the pressure of the story building.

'I didn't have many options, and usually, whenever I'm unsure about something, I ask him, so … I called him.' She shrugged as if that was the most natural thing one would do when stalking their partner – ask that same partner for advice. I burst into laughter. She was unbelievable, a one-of-a-kind person. The situation was serious, no doubt, but I couldn't help but find her somewhat entertaining. My reaction brought a smile to her face. It's always easier to laugh after the worst has passed, they say.

'And what happened next?' I admittedly couldn't wait to hear.

'He picked up and I asked him how long it took for a car engine to cool off. He asked how "on earth" I'd found myself with such random questions, and then I lost it and started yelling about how I saw him driving with another woman … Apparently, he was at home the entire time. He came to the balcony window and yelled that I was crazy. I told him to be careful with his words because, between him and me, he was the cheater, and I mercilessly gave him another chance. I hit him with the guilt bomb,' she giggled. 'Anyway, I'm positive it was him that I saw earlier, but I'll pretend I believe him this time.'

I remained silent for a moment. I didn't know, as a friend, if now was the right time to ask her the actual questions I had or simply nod supportively and perhaps throw a few offensive words at Tom every now and then as she spoke. Knowing Melissa, the latter was probably the way to go.

This dilemma was tearing at me, but I'd run out of time and needed to make a snap decision. At this, I failed miserably.

'But, if he hurt you so much in the first place, why did you give him a second chance? Didn't you think that he might do it again? And even if he doesn't, are you sure you can trust him? I don't understand why you're still with him if it only causes you stress.' I spoke honestly. 'And, forgive me for being so direct, you're cheating on him right now as well, and it's not a one-off thing either – you have an actual relationship with that guy, although he lives in a different town. In fact, you're lying to both of them. So … why don't you just finish it once and for all with Tom, stop lying to the other guy and just try to have a real thing with him, maybe?'

'Because,' her eyes popped open, looking as though I'd just asked her to eat a rat, 'Tom wronged me, and he won't get away with it by me simply leaving him. No, he will stay with me and suffer the stupidity of hurting me – the girlfriend whom all his friends adore, telling him how lucky he is to have me. Also, there is the love. I do love him still. As for the other guy, I have the right to cheat after Tom cheated on me, but I'm smarter; Tom won't know about it. In his eyes, I will forever remain the perfect girlfriend whom he hurt; I want the guilt to eat him alive. My revenge is silent, and I deserve the right to have it, so no judging please!'

Melisa and her twisted situation left me confused. As soon as I felt I was gaining some understanding of people and why they cheated, something like this would come along and throw me off completely. Pain leads to more pain. But why would love lead to pain in the first place? Is it not that people are brought together by the most beautiful feeling possible, and is that not precisely what keeps them together? How does pain find its way in? Of that, I wasn't sure. But I did know that once it did, love seemed to devolve into an agonising chain of events filled with sadness, bitterness, and betrayal. Not even a vague resemblance could be seen to the pretty picture that was painted at the beginning. The end only seemed to portray the destruction of two souls and one relationship.

I couldn't understand how Melisa could claim she loved Tom, which was why she stayed with him despite his dishonesty, yet swear she would never forgive him for hurting her and would even seek revenge on him by doing the same. Bringing her game to the next level, she wouldn't even rub her affair in Tom's face – she would do it silently for her personal satisfaction while maintaining an angel-face in front of Tom to enforce his guilt. To him, she would remain the perfect woman – good, forgiving and with the right to go crazy every now and then, someone he couldn't ever leave. She was carefully creating a personal hell for her boyfriend whom she claimed to actually love. My brain couldn't possibly digest such a concept.

June 2012

I was feeling sick, so I had to open the window for some fresh air. A long drive uphill on a curvy road is the worst experience for me. I need to be well prepared with motion sickness tablets and a portfolio of well-practised breathing exercises to avoid vomiting, but I still turn pale as a ghost anyway.

Myself and my partner at that time, Mathew, along with his good friend, Ryan, and his partner, were on our way to spend the night at the villa of said friend Ryan. It was sort of a couple's trip. Ryan and his girlfriend, Siena, had invited us for a short city break over the weekend. It sounded good, but I wasn't psyched for some reason. I didn't really know Ryan, and he gave me weird and somewhat unpleasant vibes. Between this and the car ride, I was moody during most of the journey.

My partner was excited, but I think it had more to do with his plans to secretly get stoned with Ryan, of which he thought I was completely clueless. I wished I was clueless. I wished that every time he was up to something stupid I didn't know about it or wasn't around to see. To be completely honest, I already knew this relationship wasn't going well; I couldn't see a future, and most importantly, I couldn't understand what I was waiting for to leave him. We didn't live together or anything serious like that, so nothing was stopping me, except, of course, me. Self-sabotaging was my thing. I was a master of it. I had a PhD in it. It was what I seemed best at for a large portion of my life.

The two guys had already forgotten that Siena and I existed, completely excluding us from their chat; I knew, then and there, that my evening wouldn't go much deeper than simply looking for something in common to talk about with the only other girl there. Siena actually seemed very nice, unlike her boyfriend, who had money and was arrogant about it. Actually, his parents had money, but since he was an only child and heir to the family fortune, he was spoiled beyond anything I'd ever witnessed outside of a movie.

We arrived, and of course, Ryan took us on a little show-off trip around the house, explaining where everything was bought and how much it cost. My partner loved it – I could see how impressed he was. In fact, for a moment there, I could clearly imagine him being a woman, one of those, so-called, gold-diggers. It suited him. Gosh, I knew I had to put an end to that relationship fast because I was becoming allergic to him, and everything surrounding him.

I was unpacking the toiletries from my purse when Mathew walked silently behind me. He startled me so badly that I almost dropped my face cream.

'I told you not to sneak behind me,' I said, not hiding my irritation. I was already turning back to continue with what I was doing when I noticed his expression. He had both hands covering his mouth, and his face was red – he looked on the point of bursting. 'What is it?' I asked, hoping it'd at least be funny and help cheer me up. After a minute of uncontrollable giggling, he managed to pull a normal face and speak.

'Ryan is the king. I swear, best of the best,' he stated with a smile.

'How so?' I asked – it was hard to believe.

'He's planning to play super busy all night, grilling the meat and then get himself high so he can avoid going to bed with Siena. It's genius!' he said, almost admirably.

'And why is that something he's trying to do?' I was confused. It didn't feel like something I'd label as reverently as 'genius', especially not before knowing the reason for it all.

'Listen, I'll tell you, but you have to forget you heard it, okay?' He'd lowered his voice. You'd think he was about to divulge some classified information from the FBI the way he was hushing and crouching down. I just rolled my eyes; I wasn't in the mood for drama. He continued, 'Ryan got himself an infection, some sort of sexual disease, from fucking two hookers a few weeks ago,' he stopped to laugh some more, stifling it with his hands. 'Can you believe it? He called two hookers for him and his friend, and they had an amazing night, but he caught a bug. Now he's taking medication and can't have sex before he's clean, so you need to distract his girlfriend this evening, just so she doesn't go all sweet on him and expect something tonight,'

Somewhere between his words and his giggles, I felt sick again, but we weren't driving this time, so I couldn't blame it on something so convenient. It was my shock, my disbelief at what I was hearing, and my partner's amusement at the disgusting situation. I felt very sick – I-didn't-want-to-be-there type of sick. I didn't belong there, and Mathew had no place next to me.

A couple of hours later, Siena and I were sitting comfortably with a glass of wine in hand, chatting about random things. I'd decided that wine was my only solution to get me through the evening to tomorrow, when I'd take action and sort my relationship. Siena turned out to be really pleasant to talk to; she was intelligent and ambitious, studying to be a doctor. Sadly, for her, she was very much in love with her partner, Ryan. I was trying to stay away from the topic of love and relationships, but I guess it was inevitably going to come up at some point during a girl-talk session like that.

'So how are things going with you and Mathew?' she asked, smiling as she glanced out through the window to where the guys were standing by the grill, having a chat of their own. It took a lot to resist the urge to let out a deep, heavy sigh.

'Yes, all good. You know, I mean, nothing to complain about.' My answer was all over the place. I knew I could do better than that, but Mathew's disturbing news was messing with my head. Part of me wanted to come out with it and wreck things for Ryan. Luckily, Siena didn't pay much attention to my awkward response, perhaps because she was waiting for me to ask the same question – I didn't.

'Things are great between me and Ryan as well.' She couldn't contain herself; her face was practically glowing with happiness, naïve happiness. I nodded with a forced smile, hoping that would be the end of the discussion. I tried to think of something else to talk about, but I had just one thing on my mind, the big, fat C-word: 'cheating'.

She continued, 'We've been happy for a long time now. We're coming up on three years together. I know I should be all surprised and clueless about it, but I think he's going to propose on our anniversary.' Her eyes were sparkling, and I could literally count all the teeth in her mouth from the stretched smile she had on her face.

'That's great,' I managed. I was having trouble remembering what the typical, socially acceptable response was to something like this. 'You must be very excited.'

'And what about you? Do you think you'll ever get to a place like that with Mathew?' She threw the ball to my court again. I wondered what social queues I could have possibly been giving for her to think I was enjoying the conversation and wanted to continue. I couldn't imagine a single person more ill-suited for that particular discussion than I was at that moment.

'Oh, no, no … No, I don't think so.' I shook my head and took a quick, nervous sip from my glass.

'I'm certain that Ryan and I are destined to be together; he's been just the perfect boyfriend, and my family likes him – his family adores me. It's just … meant to be.' She shrugged as if there really wasn't any other option except the one she had in her mind.

'Nice' was all I was able to say, literally biting my tongue as I reached for the wine bottle to top up my glass.

The rest of the evening was a blur to me, not because of the wine but because I was so sunken in my thoughts, trying, once again, to decipher the mystery of what made people cheat, what made them play all those ridiculously complicated games and hurt one another. I could sense my soul getting more bitter with each passing year. The more I lived to see and hear, the heavier everything felt on my chest. Was it better for Siena to know the truth and escape her delusional bubble, or did Ryan truly love her but, for him, emotions and sex didn't go hand in hand, which was why he thought it was perfectly fine to cheat?

Three months later, the news reached me by way of a friend of a friend who happened to know Siena. Apparently, Siena had eventually smelled Ryan's fat lies and had broken up with him. I was happy for her. I never met her again and didn't really know her from that time spent at the villa, but I felt relieved that the truth was finally out. She deserved it. Everyone does. But whether Mathew cheered for justice the same as me, that I did not know.

July 2012

I didn't end it with Mathew immediately. So pathetic of me. I had no excuses for postponing it. Delaying the inevitable had a high cost, which I was mercilessly forced to pay.

A weird feeling had settled in my gut, causing an uncomfortable pain of sorts, almost as if I was being warned by my own body about something I couldn't yet pin down with my mind.

The doorbell rang and I rushed to answer it. Mathew greeted me with a smile, but I could sense coldness as well. I'd been cold to him for a long time. I had my excuses, but now it was curiosity that was making me act softer. I initiated a hug and a kiss on the cheek, and that was when I felt it – a woman's perfume.

'Why do you smell like a woman?' The question popped out of my mouth before my mind had a chance to think otherwise. The truth was that, deep down, I knew the answer, but there were so many barriers muffling my inner voice that I preferred to ignore it. He laughed, a bit of a nervous laugh, but he was handling it well enough.

'It's my mother's,' he said calmly, removing his jacket. 'I went to see her before coming to yours. She was unusually sweet to me today,' he continued as I followed him silently to the kitchen. 'Do you have any coffee? I could really use a cup.' He'd switched the topic, but that only brought more questions.

'Didn't sleep well last night?' I asked while pouring some of that morning's coffee.

'I did but … By the way, I can't stay long – something came up. I can only stay about an hour,' he said while looking at his phone and taking a seat on the couch.

I put the coffee on the table and sat next to him. I kissed him passionately. He didn't expect it – neither did I. He, of course, used the opportunity to escalate things to the next level, which I didn't object to, despite how things had been between us lately.

I used to go back and analyse this moment quite a bit, or to be more clear, to analyse my behaviour. I don't do this anymore; I hardly ever think that far in the past because all lessons are already learnt from those experiences. Now I have new lessons to focus on, but I must admit that back then I had a lot to learn about myself. I knew Mathew was lying, but my ego didn't want to admit I was being cheated on, or potentially had already been replaced by someone else. I wasn't going to go through what my mother had. I was refusing to accept it.

Stubbornness can be good in some situations, but not always. In my case, I was humiliating myself, as if I had no dignity, just desperation and denial. I wanted to be the one who ended it with Mathew, in a mature way, as two adults who respected each other. But postponing it only led to him doing something I wouldn't forget, eliminating any semblance of respect I'd thought we had for each other.

I know now I shouldn't have allowed him to touch me with those dirty hands that had touched someone else right before, but back then, I wasn't thinking straight, blinded by my childhood trauma and fear that made me weak at that moment. For a few years after that day, I couldn't forgive myself for accepting his lie and, moreover, for allowing him to be intimate with me. I almost hated myself for this weakness. Now, I've reached a stage in my life where I love myself more; I've forgiven my younger self for this and other mistakes.

Getting back to July 2012, while at work, only a day after the perfume situation with Mathew, I received a surprising call from my colleague Sissi, who had the day off.

'Hey, Sissi. Is everything alright?' I asked. My initial thought was that something bad had happened; I knew she wasn't going through an easy period of her life, and to call me while I was at work and while she was supposed to be enjoying her day off was more than bizarre.

'Do you have a minute?' she asked rather seriously. She struck me as a parent who'd just found a broken vase on the dining room floor.

'Yeah, sure – oh my God, you're scaring me. Please tell me what's going on?' I said as I moved some place more private.

'Did you and Mathew break up?' she fired, giving me no time to adjust.

'What?' I asked in disbelief, my jaw already dropped and my eyes feeling as though they were going to pop out. If someone were to see me at that moment, it would have no doubt been easy for them to guess that I was in the process of receiving some shocking news. 'No! Why would you think that?' Once again the unpleasant feeling was settling on my chest, causing pain and fear.

'That's what I was worried about. I really don't know how to say this … There isn't really a good way of doing it, so I'm just going to come out with it.' She took a deep breath, meanwhile, I couldn't breathe. 'I saw Mathew today. He was holding hands with a girl. They were walking together with that sort of goofy, lovey behaviour – you know the kind. The worst part is that he saw me and greeted me as if I wasn't your friend and colleague who'd just caught him.'

I think she continued talking, or perhaps she was only asking if I was okay, but the sound was too muffled for me to make any sense of it. I remember that I knelt and started breathing heavily. Not for a moment did I question if what she'd said was true. There was no trace of doubt in my heart. I knew. I knew it all along, but I decided to ignore it. The damage was done, and even then I knew it would be a long time before I recovered to a 'normal' functioning status, and even longer until my soul would be healed completely. The feelings of betrayal, humiliation and many other emotions that were too difficult to sort through were burning me from within, and I had no idea how to stop it.

This moment would remain as the most insulting experience of my life, when an absolutely arrogant and selfish bastard, who wasn't even bothered by being caught, had the chance to humiliate me the way he did. Everyone else at least showed me kindness enough to hide it better, or beg me for forgiveness after apologising for hours. But not Mathew. Mathew made sure to step on my dignity and clean his dirty boots on it. He didn't apologise, he didn't ask for forgiveness and he didn't beg to come back. He showed no remorse.

He admitted to it and used the chance to parade around the high street of the city with his new victim, who I heard didn't last more than two months with him as he moved on to someone else. I kept on hearing about his 'achievements', and I wondered if I'd really been so blind; had he been cheating on me the entire time we were together, or did he manage to, somehow, contain himself for a time until things finally spilt over and he went for it. There are some things, some fundamental, bedrock things, one can't change, at least not without some major self-assessment and dedication – which I knew Mathew hadn't shone in our time together – and the weight of this realisation and its subsequent implication came down on me all at once.

Regardless of what exactly had gotten me into that situation, I'd repeatedly asked the universe, 'But why did it have to happen to me?' After all, it's not like I didn't know anything about cheating – my father made sure of that.

December 2013

I switched off my phone and tossed it aside. It was useless to me if I wasn't planning on talking to anyone, and I most certainly had no intention of talking. It was Christmas Eve, and a feeling of loneliness was piercing my heart. I was at my mother's home, but she wasn't there, neither was my brother, and my mother's partner was off somewhere as well. The home had no family to gather for the festive evening; it was just me, all alone. I never thought that I, as an adult, would care so much if the tradition of celebrating together on the holy night was kept or not, but judging by the stabbing pain in my heart – I did.

My brother was out of town, and my mother's partner, for years now, had always visited his relatives. Between that and the fact that he and my mother had just had another huge fight, my hopes were far from high that we would be coming together that night.

Even though my mom had been with him for many years now, she never seemed to have managed a deep connection with him. I guess some things stay broken.

An hour earlier that same evening, I saw her getting ready to go out.

'Are you going somewhere?' I asked in disbelief. She was reluctant to answer, but she had to give me an explanation – it was Christmas Eve after all.

'Yes, I'm sorry, darling, but you're going to be fine, right? I mean, you're not a child anymore. There is plenty of food in the fridge; just get comfy in bed and watch some of your favourite movies as you usually do.' She was avoiding my eyes as she continued looking for the perfect purse to match her outfit. She was beautiful, but I didn't want to compliment her.

'Where exactly are you going?' I demanded the truth. I could feel the anger starting to build up in my chest. She exhaled uneasily – it was obvious she didn't want to give me more details, but she did it anyway.

'I'm going to a friend's. Remember Jack? I mentioned him before. He's alone today, so he invited me to keep him company for a few hours. I won't be long darling.' She had an uncomfortable smile on her face as she made her way to leave, and then the door closed.

My mother always kisses me goodbye, but she didn't this time. She couldn't bring herself to do it and I knew why. She was lying to me! For a brief moment, I felt as if we'd switched roles: I was the parent and she was the teenage daughter trying to get away with something, and I had to pretend I believed her. She was cheating. It was clear to me, but I didn't feel it was my place to judge or blame. She's my mother, after all; despite how much of a grown-up I am, she will always be my parent. There was a sort of invisible barrier I didn't feel I could cross with her. I couldn't bring myself to hold her accountable for her actions, even if I considered them wrong. So I just switched off my phone, didn't touch the food in the fridge and didn't play any of my favourite Christmas movies. Instead, I decided to iron the pile of clothes lying on my bed so I would have something to keep my hands busy and my mind away from certain thoughts.

In the end, it didn't work. My thoughts had me prisoner, holding me so tight I was practically in a daze – I burnt one of my favourite shirts. There was a dark circle right on the front. I didn't get mad, I was already too upset for that. I let a big, heavy breath out instead.

Why would my mother do something like that, cheat, after having it done to her, after the pain, pain she still hadn't recovered from after many years? What was it about cheating that seemed to inevitably lure everyone to it? Does it have to do with disloyalty, or a thrill, perhaps loneliness?

I sat on my bed, holding my destroyed T-shirt, all alone on Christmas Eve with only my questions for company, questions and a growing fear. Fear of the future and what it had in store for me when it came to starting a family of my own. How lucky was I going to be?

October 2014

We'd just finished a short but nice Halloween party at the place where I was working at the time. I was making my way to the underground station when I realised I'd forgotten something, which fortunately wasn't essential; I could easily pick it up the day after, but I still stopped and wondered whether to quickly go back and get it. I was literally halfway between my work and the underground station, which made the decision even more difficult. It was one of those moments when you lose time in deciding and eventually end up going back anyway. And so I did. I rushed to the building, thinking that everyone should have been gone by that point.

When I arrived, the place had emptied, as I'd expected, but I could hear a noise over the sound of my own heavy breathing from the rush to get back. It was coming from the back exit, which we never really used, and that made the whole thing even stranger. At first, for one tense moment, I thought that someone had broken in. But I quickly tampered that fear down just as it started to rise up inside me. I eventually concluded that it had to be a colleague of mine.

After getting what I'd come back for, I didn't rush out. I was still puzzled by the noise, and admittedly, curiosity had gripped me. I headed to the back exit, not thinking to lighten my steps because I couldn't think of a reason as to why that would be necessary. Five seconds later, I thought otherwise.

I should have gone straight home and not come back at all. I should have ignored my silly curiosity. Instead, I found myself staring at not one but two of my colleagues, Jeffrey and Amy, having sex. I apologised and practically ran out of the building as if getting out of there as quickly as possible would erase the image I had in my head. I wasn't the one who'd been caught, yet I felt mortified.

As I walked to the underground station for the second time in ten minutes, my head pulsed – it wasn't pleasant. It wasn't from juicy gossip occupying my thoughts; it was the judgement I could feel myself passing. I judged Amy. I judged her harshly. She was engaged to be married soon, and she, apparently, had a crush on a colleague. More than a crush – she acted on it.

I wasn't aware if anything had ever happened between them before the party, but something had definitely happened after it. The biggest question mark I found myself facing was Amy's personality. She had this deep, forlorn look in her eyes any time I saw her. She would be from those people who do their job and mind their business, but any time I chatted with her for longer than a minute or two, her emotions came bubbling, rapidly, to the surface. Cheating aside, she didn't give the impression of someone blissfully engaged, on the edge of matrimony. In truth, she seemed quite the opposite. Of course, I never asked anything too personal – I didn't want to pry – so there was no way of knowing, for sure, if this was true or not.

I found myself sympathising with her, but even if her unhappiness was true, it still wasn't an excuse for cheating, and I admittedly did judge her for that. How could one claim that they loved, but secretly share their body with someone else? Was I wrong or did the whole world have a twisted perception of love that I wasn't aware of?

January 2015

I checked my watch. I was late for a catch-up with my friend, but just a few minutes later, his face was stretched in a smile as he saw me arriving.

'I am so sorry, Allen. Have you been waiting long?' I gave my dear friend a warm hug. I was excited to catch up with him as we were both very busy and such opportunities were rare these days.

Despite the happiness of reconnection, the full depth of his expression wasn't lost on me. He looked drained and somewhat sad.

'Not at all! Don't be silly.' He tried to look enthused, but we'd known each other for far too long for his attempt to fool me. 'Shall we?' he said, gesturing towards the restaurant where we had a reservation waiting for us.

After we got comfortable with drinks and some food, and had our fair share of general talk about unimportant things, I decided to ask my friend if everything was okay.

'Tell me, what's going on with you, and don't try to hide it because I can see it in your eyes,' I said, concerned.

'I haven't slept all night,' he exhaled. As though the lighting had changed, he suddenly looked tired, very tired.

'Why? What happened?' I reached to him and placed my hand over his.

'I had quite a wild night.' A smile spread on his face, but it twisted slightly and didn't manage to reach his eyes – there was nothing happy about it.

'Oh,' I exclaimed, confused, not sure how much of that reason was actually connected to whatever the problem was.

Allen had been in a relationship for two years at that point, but it hadn't been going well from what I'd heard. Despite his efforts to make things functional, to me, it looked like a typical toxic relationship. His partner, Susan, seemed friendly enough at first glance, but there was something sharp in her character, or at least something that didn't fit well with Allen's personality. In my eyes, this made them incompatible, but there was little to nothing I could do about it.

'I don't need to know the details of what you and Susan got up to last night,' I said jokingly, trying to dig my way to the real issue – it was clear Allen was deflecting by insinuating something sexual between him and his girlfriend. He didn't have to share if he didn't want to, but I wasn't going to take a deflection as an answer.

His face changed. I didn't think it was possible for him to look sadder, but I was proven wrong. I could sense I was close to what was truly bothering my friend.

'I'm only joking. You know you can tell me anything,' I said, pulling back a little. I wanted to give him some space, to feel comfortable.

'It wasn't with Susan.' These were Allen's only words.

For a second, both Allen and I were silent. I needed a moment to understand what he'd just told me. Had he cheated? I'd known him for years. I loved him like a brother. We had an amazing friendship that we'd both dearly appreciated throughout our time together. I always believed Allen to be a good person, and I knew he wasn't the type of man to 'get around', not when he was single and especially not in a relationship.

I battled against my shock at that moment, trying to show understanding and support for my friend. I didn't want to judge. But secretly I did. Deep down in my heart, I did judge. A little voice inside me was saying, 'If you're so unhappy, why not leave? Why did you have to cheat?' I tried to muffle the thought to try and make room for some logic.

I cleared my throat and broke the silence.

'So—' I began, but was immediately interrupted. He erupted like a volcano, as someone who'd contained pain for too long and couldn't bear it anymore. Words flew from him, and my job was just to try to follow and make sense of it.

'She is so cold towards me, so cold that I've questioned whether she has any love for me at all,' he started his confession. 'I tried talking to her about us and our relationship, about the way I feel, but every time resulted in a fight because she wouldn't listen. She'd just say that I dramatise everything – she makes me feel crazy! Then she started saying that she needed her space, which is ironic considering the fact we already don't spend much time together. She travelled twice on her own as part of this 'space' she talks about. She even mentioned that an open relationship might be good and healthy for us.' He paused for a moment just to take a breath. He seemed to be collecting himself. 'I'm positive that she's cheating on me, and so I did what I had to do.' With that, Allen finally looked up to meet my eyes. 'So last night I cheated as well.'

'Oh, Allen,' I desperately tried to shake the pitiful look I knew I had on my face, but I could feel his pain and wanted to express that to him somehow. I was torn between offering some objective, outside advice – break up with Susan – and simply comforting him. He was clearly tortured by his own feelings and actions. It was obvious he wasn't happy with what he'd done; cheating had brought him no pleasure – it only deepened his wound – yet he chose to do it over other possible solutions.

'I feel unloved, humiliated and now guilty,' he continued. He really needed to pour out his soul. I was happy to be someone he trusted enough to do that with. 'I don't see an end of this torturous cycle. At least I managed to save a bit of my dignity,' he shrugged.

'How do you mean?'.

'Well, now I can say that I hurt her, too,' he said as if that was a simple and reasonable explanation.

Allen and Susan's relationship officially continued for another few months, but it was a long, painful drag – it had died long ago. I was worried it'd take a while for him to heal his broken heart, but after only a few short months, he found the love of his life, to whom he is now married.

Apparently, when the love isn't real, which in their case it certainly wasn't – even though he was convinced otherwise – it's much easier for life to go on after things have ended. If Allen had loved Susan, despite the pain she caused him, he wouldn't have wanted to hurt her – that's what true love is – yet he purposely did just that.

I'd already had my theories and analyses on love and cheating at that point, and the whole scenario with Allen seemed fairly obvious to me, but of course, as with everything else, it's much easier when the problem concerns others and not oneself. What would I do if faced with a similar situation? That was the real question.

February 2015

'Who is he?' I asked, keeping my voice down and smiling as I caught Tessa exchanging flirty looks with some guy. We were at work, but unlike most days at work, today I was in a good mood. Tessa and I weren't particularly close, but she was a good work friend. She was in the company long before I joined, so at the beginning, she showed me around. Tessa was always polite and friendly, but she wasn't really my type of person. There was something I couldn't explain that didn't quite click with me.

Despite that, however, we were on good terms, and every now and then we would have a girly-slash-gossipy chat about what news was going around the company. Today, it seemed that she was the heart of the gossip.

'He's cute isn't he?' she answered, trying to hide her smile. 'He's in another department, but lately, he's been circling around here in his free time.' She was somewhat proud because the reason for his unusual appearance was her.

'Sounds to me like there's going to be a date,' I said. I was happy for Tessa; she was single, and if there was a spark with this guy, why not give it a go?

'I wouldn't say no to that.' She blushed.

We continued chatting in the same jolly spirit, and the work day went by. A few days later, I was out grocery shopping, and I clearly hadn't planned things well because I wound up walking home with way more than I could carry. As I stopped in the middle of the street and placed my bags on the ground to debate between rearranging the groceries to make things more manageable or simply taking the bus for what was going to be only one stop journey, I saw someone who looked familiar. That someone was a guy walking down the same street, hand in hand with a girl who also seemed familiar to me. I was never good at remembering names, but faces were my strength. The girl popped back into my mind rather quickly. She was a colleague of mine. She worked in a different department, which was why I hadn't seen much of her, and I definitely didn't know her name. But I was still having trouble placing the guy. Where had I seen him before? Then it struck me – it was the guy Tessa had been flirting with!

I grabbed my grocery bags back up and started walking. I was no longer so occupied with the dilemma between taking the bus or twisting my hands to carry the heavy bags for ten minutes. My thoughts were now thoroughly fixed on what I'd just seen, trying to digest the information. They were behaving very much like a couple, and this same guy had been showing clear interest in Tessa – she fancied him as well. So, was he lying? My life experience to that point had taught me well enough to realise that one of those two women, colleagues of mine, was being lied to, but which one was it? Or was it both? Once more, I found myself faced with the ever-puzzling question: why do people play hurtful games?

The work week was pretty busy, so I didn't have much chance to speak with Tessa, and I wasn't really sure what to speak with her about. Whatever I'd witnessed wasn't my business, and it wasn't like Tessa was a close friend of mine – the last thing I wanted to do was start putting my nose in her life. I was unsure how I wanted to approach the situation or whether I should be approaching it at all. But then an opening made itself available to me – it felt casual, appropriate. Tessa was grabbing a coffee from the vending machine just as I was about to do the same. I decided I'd say something.

'Hey, what's new with you?' I asked, rushing to get to the point.

'Well, funny you should ask.' Her eyes lit up. 'I had the best weekend, if you know what I mean.' She winked at me and gave a little side smirk.

'You didn't.' My mouth actually fell open. 'With that guy?' I asked, lowering my voice.

'Of course,' she answered, flattered by the attention and interest, which she must have mistaken as admiration from my side, but I was feeling more pity than anything else.

'But …' I had no idea how to deliver the news that he was almost certainly not single. I wasn't looking to start any workplace drama, and I definitely didn't want to be involved in it.

'Why the face?' she said. I clearly hadn't been so clever in hiding my expression.

'I just … I don't remember if we talked about if he was single or not,' I tried circling around a bit, but what I really wanted to do was scream the information I had in her face.

'He isn't single.' She shrugged as though this was obvious, unimportant, as though she'd just told me he had two brothers. 'He's dating this evil bitch, Jennifer. Actually, he's breaking up with her because she's apparently the worst. The things he told me … Honestly, I was shocked that he'd dated her in the first place. He's the sweetest; if only you could see how shy he gets when he's around me. He says it's because he likes me too much … I think I'm really falling for him.'

Tessa continued talking, and I could feel my facial expression smoothing out; I was no longer surprised or shocked. I realised that, once again, I was listening to another cheating story, complicated and ugly as they all are. It was only a matter of time before this one would end tragically for someone, maybe everyone, but right now it was still in its first stage where everything was bittersweet lies.

Two weeks later, during my break, Tessa joined me. She sat next to me and looked like she was about to explode if she didn't share whatever information she had. I could already tell that I wouldn't be happy with what I was about to hear, but I didn't feel I had much choice.

'So?' I tried to pretend to be interested.

'I just had the best, most exciting sex ever! Jennifer was away for the whole day and we spent the entire time in bed, their bed!' She laughed, which, to me, sounded reminiscent of one of those evil cartoon characters. 'I mean, don't get me wrong, they are totally not together anymore, but they're still living together. She needs to find a new place, and until then, he has no choice but to let her stay …' She spoke quickly, full of excitement, but I had to stop her. I had to be honest, to share what I knew even if it wasn't my place, which it definitely wasn't, but at this point, I felt I'd be betraying myself if I kept secret what I'd witnessed the day before.

'Tessa,' I interrupted her, 'I saw him – them – together yesterday.' My words silenced her. She was now staring intently at me, thirsty for more of what I had to say. I moved straight to the point. 'Apparently, we're neighbours. They live a few buildings down the road. I hadn't noticed until yesterday when a friend of mine was dropping me home. As we drove by, I saw them walking out, strolling down the street, holding hands. They even kissed. They looked very much together from where I was looking.'

She remained quiet, which I'd expected. It was a lot for someone in Tessa's position to absorb. I could only imagine what she must have been thinking at that moment. He'd been lying to Tessa, and his girlfriend was likely clueless about the fact that he'd brought another girl into their home, into their bed, a woman he'd gotten there with a lie. He wasn't the sweet and shy guy Tessa took him for; he was a cruel man who no doubt thought of himself as a player.

The silence didn't last for long, and the sudden arrival of Tessa's words surprised me.

'Well, he'll choose me over her – I know it. It wasn't me who destroyed my relationship and made my boyfriend look for love elsewhere. That was her. He wants me; I was in his bed, their bed, and she has only herself to blame. She lost, and I won. I don't care about anything else but that fact really.' Even though her words were arrogant and cruel, I could see pain in the little flinches on her face.

Months passed and the story didn't really evolve much further. The guy stayed with his girlfriend, and Tessa eventually lost interest in him, or at least that's what she said. However, the news of her leaving for another job came to all of us as a bit of a surprise – nobody had known she was even looking elsewhere. However, she had gotten uncharacteristically quiet some weeks before the announcement.

I felt fairly certain it was related to her drama with the guy – whom she didn't mention anymore. I never got to ask Tessa about how she felt and why the sudden change in job. Truth be told, I had a feeling she was avoiding me. I felt certain I hadn't done anything wrong, but I couldn't think of why else she'd want to keep away from me.

Tessa left, and I never saw or spoke to her again, but I did hear from a few colleagues who were closer to her that she'd started drinking heavily, which was a surprise to me. Tessa was younger than me. She was petite, had a cute face and was very amicable; it was hard to imagine her excessively drinking, but that was the rumour.

Eventually, I heard the guy she fell for, got dumped by his girlfriend, Jennifer. I wish there was a way for Tessa to know this, not for her to have another chance, but maybe it'd bring some consolation – the player was now alone because of his ugly games.

After the whole ordeal, I tried to analyse the situation, to see what I could get from it, but there were pieces missing from the puzzle. I would never know if Jennifer was really a terrible person as her now ex-boyfriend had described her, but even if she was, he had no excuse for cheating on her, especially not in such a disrespectful way, bringing Tessa into their home, into their bed. It was cruel. I'd also never know how hurt Tessa was from all that, not really – she never opened up to me in that way. I imagine I'd have been devastated if it were me.

What she had said to me only increased the size of the puzzle, 'He'll choose me over her.'

April 2016

At this point, it has been years since I last comforted my friend as she cried, broken-hearted, because of a guy whom she wasn't even in a relationship with.

Eva had really liked a guy, although he was nothing special, to me at least. He would show some interest every now and then, but most of the time he was completely emotionally unavailable, showing absolutely nothing, which Eva interpreted as 'mysterious'. She was drawn to him like a bee to honey. This honey's name was Carlos, and my friend and I used to sit for hours analysing every insignificant move he made or didn't make towards her.

At first, there was hope that he might really be into her and simply wasn't showing it as openly as she'd expected, but after a while, it was clear to me that he wasn't serious about her. It wasn't so clear to Eva. Naturally, I tried warning her, but this only made her upset; she wanted me to be supportive, so I fought my instinct to speak out and left her relationship to her. Eventually, she did get hurt.

Eva and Carlos never got truly involved – Carlos wasn't present enough for them to form any real history, at least not a deep one, but there were expectations, hope, idealised perceptions of who Carlos was, and of course, sex. After he stopped replying to her messages and completely stopped all contact with her, Eva had no choice but to finally accept the situation and move on.

None of this mattered lately, a few years later, because she was dating the love of her life, Daniel, and things could not have been better for them.

'Have a good night, guys. Have a safe journey home,' I said to them as we parted ways after a catch-up over a couple of drinks in our favourite bar.

'You too,' Daniel replied, 'and get ready for Wednesday because this one here will make you drink even more,' he laughed with a jab of his head towards Eva.

I didn't quite get what he'd meant by that, but I assumed it was some sort of a joke, so I smiled, but I'm pretty sure I wasn't convincing anyone. I quickly shifted my eyes to Eva, which only added to my confusion; she also had a smile on her face, a forced and fake one. All the while she was burning her eyes into me.

'Honey, don't say that – I won't make her drink on a school night,' she said before turning to me. 'Tell him that our girl's nights are a lot more than just cocktails.'

The air suddenly felt tense. I felt so far out of the loop yet a pressure to go along with it.

'Oh yeah, sure, of course, we always have a great girl's time.' I didn't want the moment to stretch for any longer than it already had, so I just wished them goodnight again and hurried to the taxi I had waiting for me.

As soon as I got in the car, I pulled my phone out of my purse and messaged Eva:

'What the hell was that about?'

The reply didn't come for another few minutes; I guessed she was making sure she could text back without her boyfriend seeing. I was nervously tapping my fingers on my purse when I finally received her response:

'I'm really sorry. I should have told you before, but I didn't think he'd mention anything. I swear I was planning on telling you, but he caught me unprepared.'

I still didn't understand what she was talking about, but at least we were on the same page about the fact that I had been deserving of a heads-up.

'Tell me what?'

Another long minute passed before she replied:

'I told Danny I'll be staying at yours for a night because of a late work meeting I have at the other end of the city.'

Somehow, even after a few messages, I was still feeling none the wiser.

'And are you going to stay at mine?'

My question was more rhetorical than anything else; I knew she wouldn't be staying – she would have told me a few days in advance, at least. I had a nervous feeling in my gut. I could sense that nothing good was going to come out of whatever this mysterious situation was, which was beginning to feel more and more like a destructive mess. And finally, I got a bit closer to the truth:

'I didn't know how to tell you because I was afraid you might judge me, but I'll tell you all about it tomorrow over a coffee. Okay?'

At this point, I didn't know what else to do but agree:

'Sounds good.'

Given my experience, I was ready for another cheating story over coffee, but I wouldn't have expected it from Eva. Before entering the cafe, I was still analysing, not her but myself. At this point in my journey for answers, I was beginning to feel I'd reached a conclusion: I was still too young to understand everything in life. For example, I knew I couldn't simply jump into making harsh accusations against people just because I knew being unfaithful was wrong.

My instinct and desire to judge had been pacified over the course of my investigation into the nature of cheating; my want to blame and point fingers really came from a yearning for justification, a yearning that likely started back with my dad. I then continued my search for this same justification in my friends, but I wasn't sure if I was right to do so.

Anyway, I entered the cafe ready to find a reason.

Eva was sitting, and between the expression on her face and the fact that she looked to be counting the sugar packets, I could tell she was nervous. As I approached, there was a distinctly awkward feeling between us, which after many years of comfortable friendship, was a first. She stood up to give me a hug and called the waitress over to take our order. I couldn't help but notice that she'd picked the most secluded table.

'So what's going on?' I said, smiling, after the waitress left us with two mugs of hot tea. Eva wrapped her hands around hers and leaned closer to me, speaking in a voice so low it forced me to lean in as well just to be able to hear properly.

'Do you remember Carlos?' she asked, and the way my eyes immediately widened was clearly enough of a response for her. 'Well, I ran into him on the street the other day; it was a completely random situation, really, but we stopped to chat, and then he texted me and I answered back … And I felt this old fire in me, one that never really had a proper chance to go down as everything had ended so suddenly between us. I was sure we could both feel it. I'm going to meet with him. I know I must have lost my mind to do something like this, but I just couldn't help myself. I never got over him. Never.' She looked at me, and my expression must have been harder to read now. 'Please say something.'

'Is there more?' Her story didn't feel finished yet, and I didn't want to speak before I had all the facts. I understood that some love sparks, for whatever reason, are harder to put down, and the story between Eva and Carlos clearly felt unfinished to her, which made her eager to get closure, but I had to know if that was all.

She looked away as she continued – she didn't seem to want to look me in the eyes. 'We're meeting this Wednesday.'

'I guess closure works better face to face—' I began, trying to help shoulder some of her guilt with some little justifications, but she apparently hadn't finished with her story.

'In a hotel. We're meeting in a hotel. I booked a room, which is why I told Daniel I'd be staying with you.' There it was. Now it felt like the story was properly finished. She sat there, waiting for my response, but I now had nothing to say. I needed more time to find some words that might offer some support in this delicate situation, but after a few minutes, the silence started feeling too heavy.

'You're too quiet – you're scaring me,' she said, 'but I think that's just because I'm scared of what you're going to say. All I ask, and I know it's a lot, is for you to confirm that I stayed with you should Daniel ever ask. Please?'

'Eva, honey, I'll be honest with you, I don't support you in this, but of course, I'll help you how I can,' I forced myself to reply. Eva only nodded appreciatively, but I knew she was bothered that I couldn't fully get on board.

She knew she'd crossed her moral boundaries and that she'd caught me unprepared with all this, especially after we'd known each other for so many years – she'd never done anything even remotely resembling what she was about to do. She was likely just as shocked as I was, but the excitement was drowning it out. Like a tsunami pulling back before it crashes, eventually, she would get hit by a wave of emotions. Or would she?

Not everyone felt bad about cheating; not everyone felt guilty, sad or ashamed, but there was one thing nearly everyone shared – confidence, confidence they wouldn't get caught or confidence in their decision. Otherwise, they just didn't care. Regardless of what they feel in the moment, however, the calm waters that follow the thrill almost always drudge something to the surface. I knew what Eva was about to do was wrong, there was no question about it, but I loved her dearly, and I didn't want her actions to bring her suffering. I only hoped the situation could disappear in the depths of the closet and never threaten to destroy her happiness with Daniel.

September 2017

My friend Suzi held up better than I'd ever seen anyone do under these sorts of circumstances. I admired it in a way, but I also couldn't understand it much. She'd been in a relationship for a few years, and it was the happiest she'd ever been with someone; she loved and felt loved in return. Everyone felt it, until something happened. There's always, and will always be, the little stones in the road that send one tripping, falling, and sometimes snowballing into something catastrophic. For Suzi, that was the moment when her partner, Ella, received an astounding work proposition. I was unexpectedly part of the moment as they'd invited me to their place for lunch, which quickly turned into a celebration after the phone call that brought the terrific news.

I can still remember the happiness that filled the entire room. Ella was emotional, tears on the edges of her eyes. Suzi stormed out of the flat to the nearest supermarket to get champagne. There was so much joy that day. And then, suddenly, everything started going down for them.

The work offer was flexible, giving Ella the choice between working remotely or moving to another city, which was half a day's travel from the city we all lived in. It sounded like an easy decision, which was why the choice Ella was leaning towards came as a bit of a surprise – this was when the problem started.

'I have news.' Suzi said the following week as we sat down in our favourite Italian restaurant. She was never one for subtlety or beating around the bush, but sometimes, for my sake, I wished she was. I had a feeling about what was coming – Ella's job offer was the most recent thing, so it was easy to connect the dots. Despite that, I still had a sharp feeling climbing up within me. 'I'm moving. I mean, we are; Ella prefers it over the remote work,' Suzi shrugged. You'd think she'd just made an order off the menu and not a major life decision.

'Is she sure about that?' I asked in disbelief, but I had the feeling that the answer was set, firm and unpleasant to hear as it was. I had to be happy for my friend, but something didn't feel right.

'Hell yes, more than anything else. She's glowing. I'm not happy to have to move, but watching her gets me excited.' She sounded like she was trying to convince me, to convince herself, but it was right there in her words – she wasn't too happy about it.

Suzi was the adventurous type, so it wasn't hard to imagine her embracing life in a new city, but she was also someone who was deeply connected to their roots; family and friends meant the world to her. All in all, I knew this decision wasn't as light as she was making it sound.

'Have you discussed it? I mean, if you don't feel fully comfortable with this decision, why doesn't she consider working remotely for a bit?' My question felt logical to me, like something any couple would do – discuss and make a decision together. But I had a feeling, a little voice whispering to me, that this wasn't how things had played out.

'We have discussed it, of course. I told her I don't feel ready for such a step, but she insisted on moving, even if it's without me, so …' She exhaled deeply and ran her hands through her hair, giving her true stress away. 'I don't have much of a choice, do I?'

'What are you talking about? Of course you do …' The sharp feeling had turned into some kind of sympathy nausea, if there was such a thing; I couldn't believe what I was hearing. The situation was way more serious than I'd suspected. Not only was a big change coming for both Suzi and Ella, but it seemed like Ella had crowned herself as the one who got to make the final decision; she did so when she made it clear that she wasn't bothered leaving Suzi behind. It's rather cruel to make someone follow or otherwise live without you, especially when there's an option that would make things fairly easy for both parties.

'I can't be without her. I love her too much. It's *that* simple.' This was all Suzi said.

Two weeks later, Suzi showed up at my door with a bottle of wine in hand and a smile on her face, which looked painful for her to maintain – it did a better job of giving her suffering away than covering it.

'Come in,' I said, still surprised by the unexpected visit. My door is always open to my friends, but that doesn't make seeing them like this any less shocking.

'I'm sorry to come unannounced, but Ella and I might be breaking up, so I'm in desperate need of a drink, and I can't be alone.' Suzi took off her shoes in one quick move and headed for the kitchen, straight to the cupboard with wine glasses.

I slowly turned the key to lock the door, frightened by what I had just heard; I could only imagine the pain Suzi was in. She seemed visibly calm and spoke as if nothing had happened, but the truth was that any moment now she was about to collapse into pieces – her entire world was falling apart. I shook off the unpleasant feeling of something dreadful coming; I had to be in the best possible shape to help my friend, who was about to go through what could possibly be the darkest time in her still very young life. I joined her quickly and helped with pouring the wine.

As I sat down and waited for her to start talking, I noticed the dark circles under her eyes, eyes that were now red, perhaps from sleepless nights, or countless tears. It pained me to see Suzi like this – she was normally so full of life.

'I started making plans for after we move – you know me and how I love planning,' she said as she finally sat down opposite me. 'Ella said it would be better if she went first, on her own for the time being, maybe a couple of months. She said she wanted to see how she liked it and that I could probably join her after that.' Suzi was making short gasps between each sentence as if it was difficult for her to speak. 'I said that I'd prefer to be there with her from the very beginning, and she asked me if I was sure I wanted to go at all … There was no option in which I don't go, I told her, but she just kept asking if I was sure, going on about how it was too big of a step for me and that I'd have to find another job, make friends and settle. I told her that was my concern, not hers, and that I'm happy to do it as long as I could be with her, but she just kept repeating her question, again and again and again, as if …'

'As if she wanted you to say that you didn't want to go.' It felt like an act of sympathy to complete that sentence for her. Whether this was more for her or for me, I don't know.

'Exactly,' Suzi confirmed. She looked as though she'd just put something bitter on her tongue. 'I told her that she knows how much I love her and that I'd go anywhere for her, for us. But she said … She said …' Suzi's voice broke. It was clear she wouldn't hold for much longer. 'She said that if I wanted to do it for some other reason, I could, but if that was my only reason for going, I better not …' Her cry ended the sentence.

I moved over to her and wrapped my arms around her shoulders. My chest ached for her. Suzi's pain was so pure and honest – it came right from the heart, the soul, so deep and innocent that she resembled a child who'd fallen, crying over a bleeding knee. Love was complicated; rather, people were – I've seen more tears from pain than I have from the joy love was supposed to bring. Did that make love dangerous in our hands, then, and not the overestimated 'best feeling' a person could experience? Too many thoughts and questions, and almost no answers.

One week later, I received a message while at work. It was from Suzi.

'I'm in a bar and there's a super hot girl at the table across mine. I'm thinking of trying my luck. What do you say?'

I was busy and couldn't be seen on my phone, but this felt like a bit of an emergency, so I snuck out for few minutes.

'Aren't you at work?'

She replied immediately:

'I called in sick, which isn't entirely a lie. I'll send you the address of the bar – come join me.'

I wanted to go just to get her out of there, and remind her that she needed to get a straightforward response from Ella about whether she still loved her and saw a future together. I'd already told her this a couple of times at this point, but she only met me with resistance. I didn't blame her. If she didn't ask, she could avoid fully accepting things; it would become much more real once she had an answer to those questions.

'I'm at work. I can't join you. Go home, Suzi, please. You'll only make things messier.'

Even though I wanted to help, but couldn't at the moment, I knew she was the one who had to make a decision. I waited. She didn't reply. I worried she was already doing something stupid with a random person, which would lead nowhere helpful for anybody, so I sent another message:

'Listen to me, Suzi, you're not thinking clearly. If you do something now, you'll regret it.'

Another brief pause followed, and I wondered if I'd already lost her or if she was actually contemplating what I was telling her. After a very long minute, I finally received a reply:

'Do you think Ella has someone else already? I wouldn't be surprised. No harm if I'm only cheating back, right?'

I took a deep breath. We'd been over this, and other possible theories, in recent conversations. I had also expressed how wrong I felt it was for Ella to put Suzi through this ambiguous emotional torment rather than be honest about whether or not it was over between them, that they'd shared many nice moments but it was time to part ways. A conversation like this would be painful, no doubt, but it would be the honourable thing for Ella to do. Suzi deserved a clean break, but Ella wasn't delivering it. Instead, there would be hopes and kisses one day and uncertainty with tears and pain on the next. Day after day, a painful rollercoaster of emotions. Suzi, meanwhile, was living in a state of active contradiction – she was ready to cheat, yet she almost seemed to hold Ella in higher regard, as though her name were some holy object, beyond reproach. This made things more difficult for me.

'She is responsible for her actions, and you for yours! Please don't do anything you'll regret. I have to go back to work. I'll text you later.'

As I arrived home that evening, I already knew Suzi was safe at her own home, away from trouble. Most importantly, I knew she was there with no reasons for regret.

Another week later, the winds had shifted. Suzi called sounding like a different person; she was in a good mood.

'Let's go shopping. What do you say?' she offered.

'Shopping?' I had to repeat to make sure I understood correctly. Suzi wasn't the type to go shopping recreationally. This in combination with the excitement in her voice was enough for me to feel there was something weird going on. 'Do you need something specific?'

'Actually, I do, yes; I'm in need of some sexy lingerie.'

'Oh,' was all I could say. I didn't expect this answer, but I suspected it was related to her good mood. The situation with Ella and Suzi wasn't sorted yet – it seemed like there was some dramatic new change every day.

'I know what you're thinking,' she said rather loudly, 'but the truth is that I'm not giving up. I will fight for this relationship because it feels right; I know that this person is my future … I will do everything I can. So, are you coming shopping with me, or what?'

Her reply sounded more like a statement, a well-rehearsed statement, in fact. It felt like she was saying it partly for her own motivation. But I did find inspiration in it – I shouldn't give up on my friend. I wouldn't let Ella, who was too afraid to make a firm decision, continue to toy with Suzi's heart. At least that's what I thought, but the truth of the matter was that I was tired; I felt drained from my effort to reason with Suzy – there's only so much someone outside of the situation can do. So, I was just going to be supportive, in whatever she wanted to do.

'Sure, I'll come with you.'

That evening, I was setting myself up for a cozy night in, a glass of wine and a book already in my hands. Suzi was going to have her wild night, according to her plans, and although I doubted it would improve the overall situation, I was hoping for a miracle. As I turned to my spot in the story – I was roughly halfway through a new crime novel, and it was really starting to get its hooks in me – my phone rang. It was Suzi. As much as I was doubting that her plan would mend everything, the call was still unexpected.

'Hello?' I said, not bothering to keep my finger in my page.

'Do you want to hear something interesting?' Suzi's question was rhetorical, barely even a question – more of a jabbing comment. She sounded like she was in pain. I'd actually stopped breathing for a moment at the sound of her. 'Ella never came home. She called just a few minutes ago to tell me that work had asked her to come out for a few days, something urgent. She was happy to do it, of course, and left without even saying goodbye.'

'Oh god, Suzi …' I could only guess at the effect that must have had on her emotional state at the time, but I had to try and console her. 'It wasn't right of Ella to leave without waiting for you and explaining first, but it's just for a few days and then she'll be back. You still have two weeks before the official move, so there's plenty of time to talk yet, and hopefully agree to the idea of moving together. Everything will be fine …'

Sadly, I was wrong. Ella never came back. Eventually, she asked Suzi to finish packing her belongings and send them out. That was the most heartbroken I'd ever seen anyone. Ella and Suzi's split up was definite, without a goodbye, without much explanation as to why it happened how it did, after years of being together. I never got to know if there was someone else or if Ella simply grew tired of their relationship. Suzi tried healing her heart with a lot of alcohol and the beds of different people, but none of it helped – she was only devastating herself further.

It took Suzi two years to get back to her old self, to which she'd added an admirable strength. But it will take a lifetime to understand why some people hurt those whom they love. And I'm afraid the answer may never be clear.

October 2018

I was sitting on the sofa, speechless, with a soup of mixed emotions bubbling inside me. I had just received a message and then a phone call, from different people, and each had left me puzzled and worried.

Ten minutes ago ...

My phone gave a *ping*, pleasantly chirping out that I'd received a text. For a moment, I thought I might leave it for later as I was occupied with my book – a different book – and wanted to finish my chapter before getting busy with my day, but curiosity overtook me. The message was from my friend Nikki, and my eyes opened wider than I thought possible after reading:

'Honey, don't panic, I'm in the hospital, but I'm fine.'

I reread the message to make sure I wasn't, somehow, missing something, and then immediately called her. She didn't pick up, but she texted a reply:

'I can't talk at the moment, but I'm better now. I promise.'

I still couldn't believe this was happening. I didn't even know what was happening, but I couldn't believe it. As much as I was relieved that Nikki seemed to be fine, I needed more information:

'But what happened? What hospital are you in? Let me visit and bring you something. Do you need anything?'

Her response was quick:

'I had a little accident and hurt myself, but I'm all better now, and I'm not alone – Luke is here. He'll take me back home and look after me until I recover.'

Unexpected news had struck me a second time within minutes, but I hid my shock, which is, thankfully, significantly easier to do over text. I reassured her that I'd be there for her if she needed me and asked her to call me as soon as she felt well enough. Our chat ended there, but it left me feeling anxious and confused.

I knew Nikki well, and I was aware of the personal hell she'd been living in for the past two months; her long-term partner, Luke, suggested that they take a break, but to me, this all seemed like he was just trying to get a bit of distance for when the real drama started, when he'd finally admit that he wanted to end the relationship. From where I stood, it looked like he was doing everything possible to show Nikki that their relationship was heading for the end: he was consistently cold to her and he came home late every night to, I assumed, avoid talking to her in the home they'd shared, where she'd moved to live with him. His promotion at work helped a lot with the avoidance efforts as part of the job required him to travel for a couple of days here and there.

A little over a month before this hospital situation, he'd told Nikki that he thought it would be best if they temporarily gave each other space, which meant that he needed her to move out. Meanwhile, Nikki swore to me that he had been acting mysterious lately, particularly when it came to the phone; he would talk in a hushed voice and sometimes take his calls out in the garden, and he always had a smile on his face when he came back inside.

For me, it felt all too obvious that he'd found someone else and simply lacked the courage to break up with Nikki because she'd been part of his life for seven years; their families knew each other and, most importantly, Luke and Nikki were engaged. Not that any of that had stopped him from having a little something on the side, or maybe accidentally finding true love, whatever one might want to call that situation.

As I've mentioned, I'd since given up on judging and labelling. Firstly, this was because of my own inability to accurately understand these situations, no matter how much of my life I'd spent searching out the answers. Second, I'd since lost faith in my ability to be objective on these matters. I'd noticed that I didn't hesitate to call the person in question a disrespectful pig if they were hurting one of my friends, but when the perpetrator *was* a friend, I would try to look for justification, even if I felt it was wrong. So I started learning how to simply accept things as they came. My mantra became 'If someone doesn't want to be with you, simply let them go, heal and move on.' Right? Of course, it's a lot easier said than done, and I would include myself among the numbers of those who struggled with this.

At first, when Nikki started sharing the wreckage of her relationship, I suggested that she save her dignity and leave him because of how disrespectful he'd been to her instead of being honest, which she deserved. She refused to do so. This wasn't a surprise to me; after all, nobody takes such steps lightly. She loved him, which made sense, and it also meant she was willing to try and save their relationship.

When Luke finally asked her to give him some time alone, no doubt hoping she would take the hint, pack her luggage and move out, she instead packed only a small bag, just enough for her to stay over her parents' place, a few hours out of the city, for a month or so. I was shocked that she compromised so much, but it was what she wanted, securing herself a month away from work and travelling back home to patiently wait for her partner to get over whatever was occupying him. I admired Nikki's strength for that, to some extent, but another part of me, admittedly, thought of her as weak.

'I love him too much, and I want to save our relationship, so yes, I would forgive him if he cheated on me,' she said to me, leaving me speechless, something that was no longer foreign to me. Nikki was determined not to lose Luke – she was ready to do what was necessary.

After a month of freedom for him and silent torment for her, Nikki returned to their home so she could resume her work and life. Luke met her with the final decision he had made, which was that he wanted her to move out and for them to remain separated for the time being. This news was not what she was hoping for nor what she'd expected as she was convinced that the space she'd given was more than adequate, but to me, this wasn't surprising at all. What was surprising was when she called me, sobbing, saying that she'd found a used condom in the bathroom bin while packing her things – the bastard didn't even clean before she got back.

I was disgusted. I would have never been able to believe that someone who was otherwise so charming and intelligent could disrespect someone on this level, had I not heard the stories myself.

Luke had helped her find a new flat – I imagine he felt it would clear a bit of his conscience. He even helped organise movers for her things. I'm pretty sure she interpreted these things as signs of care, but to me, it only felt like he was trying to get rid of her sooner.

And so there I was, sitting on my couch with my phone still in my hand and a book going unread at my side; just three days after Nikki had been on her own, she was now in the hospital. My heart ached, wishing I could do more for her.

Then I received a call. At first, I thought it was Nikki calling back already, but a quick glance at my phone proved otherwise; the screen displayed a name I didn't recognise – 'Jenn'. I didn't know a 'Jenn'. I stared at the phone for a few seconds, trying to recall some key piece of identifying information, before finally deciding to answer. But as soon as I heard the voice on the other end, it all clicked. It was Jenn, Luke and Nikki's neighbour. I'd met her twice, once at a garden party and another time for dinner. She was more gossipy than I could generally handle, but she was sweet and genuine, so I didn't mind exchanging numbers with her.

This was the first time Jenn had ever called me, which felt weird, but it also brought a sense of urgency – what brought her to the point of calling me instead of one of her closer friends?

'I'm so sorry to bother you, really, but I don't have much information at this point and I wanted to make sure Nikki was okay, so I thought, as her good friend, you must know something,' she said, cutting straight to the point.

'Oh, you know about that?' I didn't manage to hide my surprise; I myself had only learnt about Nikki a few minutes ago while Jenn, on the other hand, seemed to have known for longer. I had no idea how she could have found out.

'Of course I do!' She exclaimed, as though this should have been obvious. 'I saw Luke storming out of his house as I was getting out of my car. He was pale and looked worried, so I had to ask. He told me something happened to Nikki and that he was going to her place to pick her up and then straight to the hospital. Poor girl. I just hope she's alright.'

I listened intently and started feeling some pieces of the puzzle sliding into place, but the whole situation was beginning to feel more bizarre by the second. And it seemed I wasn't the only one looking for answers.

'She is much better now, or at least this is what she told me earlier. But hang on, you said that Luke went to pick her up first?' The beginning of this story was not clear to me at all.

'Yeah, I found it weird too. Why didn't she call an ambulance instead of him, but …' her voice changed, feeling tighter somehow. I felt my stomach tense. 'Well, Nikki has always seemed like this perfect girl, you know? And they've always seemed so happy, the perfect couple, if such a thing existed, but things seemed to have changed recently. I've heard them fighting, a lot. Once the yelling got so loud I felt to look out through my kitchen window to see if I could see anything, to check in. Nikki sounded mad, and I saw her throwing something at him, as if to hurt him. A minute later he stormed out of the house. Forget trouble in paradise, this looked like hell – not that I want to be gossiping or anything, but you know, when it's right there in front of your eyes it's hard to ignore sometimes.'

She was going on and on, saying things I hadn't the slightest clue about, but I couldn't imagine why Jenn would make something like this up – she was a gossip, not a liar. I was beginning to feel as though I didn't know my own friend. Surely, she would have shared something like this with me. I needed to know more, and thankfully, Jenn seemed happy to continue.

'I never pictured her being the aggressive type,' she went on. 'She's so tiny, sweet and polite, but I swear, there were moments when I was concerned for Luke – I hardly ever heard his voice, only hers. I don't know much, but I haven't seen Nikki around recently. I didn't want to get nosy and ask where

Nikki was, so I just left it, but I got my answer soon after that.

'One day, Luke returned home holding hands with some girl. Never seen her before – no idea who she was, but she was pretty, of course. They got out of his car. It was broad daylight, but this didn't stop him from holding her hand and walking her straight into the house. He clearly didn't mind being seen, so I'd assumed that he and Nikki had broken up. Then just when I thought I was done being surprised, Nikki came back from wherever it was she went.

'She seemed to pretend everything was fine; told me she went to visit her parents. She gave no hint that anything else was going on. I felt the urge, you know, woman to woman, to warn her about what I saw. If Nikki was still part of Luke's life, that made him a cheater. She had a right to know, I thought, but I didn't think it was my place to say anything, so I didn't. Then a few days later, I saw her loading her luggage into Luke's car. I saw her through my kitchen window again, and this time she saw me as well. She smiled and waved; she didn't look at all like she was saying goodbye. You know what I mean? If you're leaving for good, you can at least make the effort to knock on my door and say something like 'keep in touch', anything really, but she only smiled, as if she was going grocery shopping and would be right back. I didn't pay much attention at the time because, obviously, I was saddened by the whole thing and the apparent outcome – it's never nice to see a couple falling apart. But today … Today when I saw Luke rushing to get to Nikki and bring her to the hospital, I had a crazy thought. Crazy!'

Jenn paused for the first time in minutes. She apparently needed to take a breath after all the talking, which I was grateful for because it gave me a second to process all the information. I felt like I was learning about some secret life, like something you hear about on TV or in movies. How had I never noticed anything before? I felt a little bit bad as well – it did feel a little like gossiping – but I couldn't stop Jenn now. I had to know.

'What crazy thought?' I almost whispered.

'Well, maybe it's not that crazy. It's not unheard of for someone to think that injury leads to sympathy.' She didn't say it outright, but I followed.

'Are you suggesting that Nikki did something to herself to get back with Luke?' I felt gross just saying it. This, after all, wasn't a movie. This was real life, but something like this felt too far from reality. It was insane to even think of it.

'Well, people get desperate when they're losing something dear to them, and despite their problems, I'm sure he was dear to her. She was excited to start planning their wedding, and then her whole future got destroyed just a few days ago when she moved out. So, I wouldn't rule it out – she easily could have made up an injury or even actually hurt herself to get his attention back on her. I wouldn't be surprised. It wouldn't be the craziest thing I've heard someone do out of love.' The way Jenn ended sounded as casual as though she'd just told me what she'd gotten up to that day.

'You never know …' I, on the other hand, was having trouble taking this all in. I didn't know what to make out of it or even how to begin understanding it. Why would Nikki not tell me she was fighting with Luke? Then again, if she was the reason for those fights, would she be in a position to say anything? After all, maybe Luke wasn't growing cold so much as being pushed away, if what Jenn said was true. Although, I had to admit it made more sense that Nikki would be so ready to forgive Luke if she, too, had something to feel guilty about. But still, for her to hurt herself to get Luke back was ridiculous.

After a couple of days, I finally got Nikki on the phone; her voice sounded cheerful, not at all as I'd expected. I was no doubt the one who sounded weird now, playing it cool as I prepared to find out what I could; meanwhile, theories and suspicion buzzed around my mind.

'I'm just fine, sweety. Believe me, Luke is taking such great care of me. He's been wonderful, honestly. He's even cooking for me – he does everything. I can't complain at all.' She said and at least I knew she was okay.

'But, what happened? I still don't have any idea how you wound up in the hospital in the first place. Was it serious? Are you in pain?' I had so many questions that I couldn't help but fire them off one after the other.

'I really don't want to get into it now. I'll just get upset and I don't want that. But as soon as I got hurt, I called Luke, and he came immediately – he was so sweet. He stayed with me the entire time I was in the ER. Honestly, I'm so lucky to have him – he is just precious. And no, I'm not in much pain; the doctor prescribed me some pills.' She sounded so laid-back, as though we were out for coffee, and there I was worried and confused.

'So you're staying over at … his house?' I hesitated to ask – that place was also hers up until recently.

'Yes, I am. He insisted that I stay so he could keep an eye on me.' She was satisfied, happy. For her, the focus of the conversation wasn't even her health but her success at re-establishing some semblance of peace with Luke.

We didn't chat much longer as she said she was feeling drowsy from her medication, but I promised to call her in a few days to check back in.

After nearly a week, during which I was feeling particularly exhausted from work, I finally sat on the sofa with a cup of tea, ready to call Nikki. I'd been thinking about her almost constantly, trying to unravel the mystery, refusing to accept that she would intentionally create such an unfortunate situation.

'How are you doing, love?' I asked as soon as she picked up.

'Honestly, you're not catching me at the best time.' Her voice sounded completely different from our last conversation.

'What is it?' I was getting worried. I didn't know if something was wrong with Luke or her health. I hoped it was the former.

'Luke just told me that since I'm doing better that it was about time I went back to my own place.' She sounded both irritated and sad, understandably so.

'Well, that makes sense, right? I mean, it was very nice of him to offer help – it was an honourable and humane thing to do – but it wouldn't have meant that things had gone back to how they were before, I imagine.' This all sounded logical enough to me, but this didn't seem to be the case for Nikki.

She remained silent, which I knew likely meant that she was irritated by the unpleasant reminder. Then again, for all I knew, she could have been letting it sink in, accepting the reality. In any case, I decided to use the silence to try and lay down some more reason.

'Nikki, darling, he cheated on you! Luke was with another woman in the house while you were away at your parents' place. Jenn saw them going in together, holding hands, literally days before you returned. He disrespected you, and now the important thing is that you respect yourself. Please, step away from this dead-end situation. It's for your own good. I'm begging you.'

Nikki didn't interrupt me, nor did she jump in immediately after I'd finished. After a few long seconds, which stretched quite long, she finally replied.

'I thought, considering my circumstances, maybe things would change. I thought he would want me back, but I guess I was wrong.'

The conversation didn't last much longer after that. Nikki hurried to get off the phone because she needed to pack her things. It was, after all, time for her to go. She promised to call back once she'd settled a bit more, and then she hung up, and I was left alone, alone with my grasping thoughts, trying to make sense of things.

She'd clearly hoped her accident would bring about some change between her and Luke. Jenn's theory was getting harder to ignore – it was pushing up inside of me despite my efforts to shove it down. Had she really hurt herself? Was it love that was capable of such a terrible thing, or was it people?

At some point later in my life

At first, I thought it was love, the real kind, because it wasn't like anything I'd felt before. Now, years later, I've come to the realisation that it wasn't love but an obsession. I had been making more of us than what we actually were. Now that we're no longer together, the fog that had been blurring my mind has since lifted, and I can see. There were so many warning signs that I seemed determined to ignore, in the name of my strong beliefs, in the name of the expectations I made up. It was as Ada Limon had so beautifully put it: 'How funny that I called it love and the whole time it was pain.' I could now relate without the slightest hesitation. Although there's no cheating involved in this story, not in the traditional sense, I could say I cheated on myself. I stopped being loyal to me and, instead, I prioritised him – a personal betrayal that cost me dearly.

None of it was his fault – it was all mine, mine for seeing something non-existent and wrapping my dreams and hopes around it. There was also an element, the desire, of 'fixing someone broken'. As one might have gathered from these stories, I was weirdly drawn to people who needed help. I would put all my energy into helping them instead of working on myself, which was the real problem.

Can there be real happiness in a relationship between two people in need of fixing if only one is helping, loving and caring while not receiving the same in return, leaving them drained, empty and desperate? Hope, when used properly, is a powerful tool, and misplacing it cost me a great deal of pain. I tried harder than I thought I was capable, I coped with more than I thought possible, and in the end, I'd given so much of myself that I couldn't even feel myself anymore. I was slowly disappearing just because I didn't want to give up on the ridiculous obsession with love that I'd attached to that person.

This kind of obsession behaves more like an addiction than anything else, and it's equally as hard to break out of, and when things finally ended, it wasn't the lost love I suffered from but the idea of a future I no longer had.

During the relationship, the bottom line was that I felt hurt. I even thought he might have been cheating on me and that was the reason things weren't going the way I wanted them to, but soon after, I realised that his heart just never opened for me, not really. What feels more painful - knowing that someone loved you and then stopped loving you or that someone never loved you at all? The more I stayed, the more hurt I was, and the more I didn't want to let it go. I did the impossible, pushing my limits, breaking my limits – less the 'impossible' and more the 'shouldn't have been'. I'd even agreed that he didn't have to change the way he was or how he felt as long as he stayed with me. I was desperate for the love of the one who didn't love me.

After some deep self-analysis, I realised I was drawn to rejection – the more lack of affection there was, the harder I would try to make it work. It was as though I didn't know how to accept actual love and care; I only recognised and responded to the opposite. It sounds twisted, I know, but what it all comes back to is my father – I was traumatised. He abandoned his family – he abandoned me – to chase what turned out to be nothing more than another fling for him. I thought he didn't love me anymore, at least not enough to stay.

While I was growing up, he had the decency to stay in touch, showing care from time to time, but it felt like charity to me. I didn't want a piece of his love – I wanted it all.

Now, in my adult life, I've reached the conclusion that I've been operating within a pattern consisting of unhealthy relationships that aren't based on what I deserve but on my trauma, my need for love from those who have no real interest in me. My last relationship ended with my realisation that I had been forcing myself on a person who didn't want me, a person who was ready to let me go at any second, a person who never even managed to say 'I love you', just like my father never did. It made me all the more desperate for this person's attention. I'd become obsessed with the idea of making him love me, stubbornly holding onto the illusion I had of our relationship.

All this ended when I finally said, '*I want better for myself.*' As hard as it was to go against the damaged instinct I had, I finally, for the first time in my life, took the step and said, '*Enough.*' I closed a page of my life full of mixed emotions, and I turned over a new blank one, ready to see what else life had in stock for me.

To love and respect myself turned out to be empowering indeed.

EPILOGUE

Even after so many years of adulthood, personal experiences, and so many other experiences I'd heard about, I still don't think I can confidently say I quite understand why cheating happens, under what circumstances it happens and how people really feel about it. The majority of people say it's the worst thing someone can do to their partner, an act of betrayal, selfishness and a complete lack of morals. But again, many of those who would say this have cheated as well. Keeping one's private actions secret allows them to publicly display the opinions they believe are more acceptable by society's standards, meaning that the morals often preached are, in fact, fake. The truth comes from personal experiences that require courage to say out loud.

Rules, like *you have to be faithful to your partner*, are being bent because everyone thinks their circumstances are unique, justifying a little step off the straight path. Old passion or a new fling, lack of love or careless instinct, a little mistake or discovering one's true love – the list of reasons, excuses, and justifications goes on and on. And yet there isn't a single word that can unite it all into one clear answer to the question *'What makes people cheat?'*

After so many years, I've finally decided to stop chasing this question. Perhaps the answer really is unique to every person, and perhaps it's time for me to let the past go. My circumstances with my own family – my inspiration for this whole journey – now feel less heavy than they had throughout all those years when I carried disappointment, rage and pain along with this question. Free from those emotions, I now feel ready to leave it all behind and start fresh.

It feels good.

NOTES

<u>Varma et al., 2023</u>

Why do people prefer to betray their partner rather than exercise the choice they have to end their relationship and start a new one? It's an interesting question. There are different opinions about what leads to the act of cheating and what represents this act, ranging from a touch or a kiss to sexual intercourse.

The definition of infidelity, according to academics, is a hidden act that violates the agreement between two individuals that certain needs will not be met by anyone else outside of their relationship.

In some cases of infidelity, studies support the idea that the reasons could be due to a lack of something in the relationship, although research has shown that relationship satisfaction tends to play a relatively small role in such cases.

One factor that has been linked to infidelity, according to research findings, is low self-control. Individuals predisposed to it have a greater tendency to engage in sexual behaviour outside of their relationship. Men, compared to women, have a higher chance of engaging in unfaithful behaviour, according to recent studies.

Dissatisfaction, neglect and anger are also accepted as reasons for why an individual might participate in infidelity. For example, studies have found that living separately or a severe absence of affection and attention can all be influential to an individual's decision to engage with a third person. Moreover, in cases where one finds out that the other has cheated, it is very likely that anger can potentially trigger revenge, leading to reciprocal cheating.

Additionally, situations assuring confidentiality can affect one's decision to participate in extramarital sex, and studies have shown disturbingly high figures of infidelity prevalent in dating relationships.

<u>Rosenberg, 2018</u>

Infidelity is characterised by breaking the commitment of sexual exclusivity, and reasons for it could be uncontrollable impulses for love and lust. Such actions generally lead to separation or divorce, but the emotional and mental impact can be so intense that it can lead to suicide, homicide and other 'crimes of passion'.

Despite the global acknowledgement of the destructive power of infidelity, 50% of individuals in committed relationships cheat, 20% of monogamous and married individuals are unfaithful, and many think of it but keep their thoughts private.

While someone might be open with their partner about many things, thoughts and actions of unfaithfulness usually remain unspoken.

Scientists argue that love and sex can actually be seen as an addiction, meaning that the human brain gets addicted to receiving both.

Cheating affects people of all socioeconomic groups, races, religions, sexual orientations and marital arrangements.

While sexual infidelity applies to anything from a kiss to intercourse, there is such a thing as *emotional infidelity,* described as a strong emotional bond, including sexual tension, with someone who isn't a partner, and this is just as damaging as sexual infidelity can be. In fact, affairs that include both sexual and emotional bonds are proven to be the most powerful.

According to studies, heterosexual men worry mainly about sexual betrayal whereas heterosexual women consider emotional infidelity just as damaging as sexual infidelity. Studies show that homosexual men and women are equally distressed by both emotional and sexual infidelity; however, this is significantly less in comparison to heterosexual men and women.

<u>Sharpe et al., 2013</u>

In an experimental study exploring how cheating experience influences one's perception of infidelity, participants were asked how 'acceptable' and 'forgivable' they considered the unfaithful action of the person in a hypothetical scenario they were presented with. Men and women with previous betrayal experience tended to justify the unfaithful person, whereas participants with no cheating experience found the unfaithful act as overall unacceptable.

REFERENCES

Rosenberg, K. P. (2018). *Infidelity: Why men and women cheat*. Hachette UK.

Sharpe, D. I., Walters, A. S., & Goren, M. J. (2013). Effect of cheating experience on attitudes toward infidelity. *Sexuality & Culture*, *17*, 643-658.

Varma, P., Barman, J. D., & Maheshwari, S. (2023). Why Did I Cheat on My Partner? Mapping the Motives of Infidelity in Dating Relationships Through the Perpetrators. *The Family Journal*, 10664807231201629.